Uncl Is Tricky!

Written by Jill Eggleton
Illustrated by Brent Chambers

Rigby

One day, the twins came
home from school.
They saw a truck
at their house.

"Uncle Ted is here,"
they shouted.

Uncle Ted put
a mask on.

“Hi, Uncle Ted,” said the twins.
“You look like a bear.”

"I **am** a bear,"
said Uncle Ted, and
he ran after the twins.

Uncle Ted liked to play
tricks on the twins.
He put worms in their socks.

The twins put on their socks.
“**Yuck!**” they said.

The twins ran after
Uncle Ted with the worms.
But he was too fast.

"We will play a trick
on **you**," they said.

"You can't," said Uncle Ted.

After dinner, Mom said,
"We will have some ice cream.
Uncle Ted likes ice cream."

The twins got some salt.
They put it all over
the ice cream!

Uncle Ted saw the ice cream.
"I love ice cream,"
he said.

He got a big spoon
of ice cream.

“**Yuck! Yuck! Yuck!**”
said Uncle Ted.

The twins laughed
and laughed.
Uncle Ted laughed, too.
"OK," he said.
"**You** played a trick on **me**!"

Instructions – A Trick

You need:

1

Put the eggs
in a pot of water.

2

Cook the eggs.
Cut the tops off.

3

Get all the egg
out of the shells.

4

Put the shells
in the eggcups.
Put the shells
upside down.

Kids!
Get an adult to help you with this trick!

Guide Notes

Title: Uncle Ted Is Tricky!
Stage: Early (3) – Blue

Genre: Fiction
Approach: Guided Reading
Processes: Thinking Critically, Exploring Language, Processing Information
Written and Visual Focus: Instructions, Speech Bubbles

THINKING CRITICALLY

(sample questions)

- What do you think this story could be about? Look at the title and discuss.
- Look at the cover. Why do you think the twins have purple paint around their eyes? Why is Uncle Ted laughing?
- Look at pages 2 and 3. Why do you think the twins are happy to see Uncle Ted?
- Look at pages 4 and 5. Why do you think the twins aren't frightened of Uncle Ted, even though he is wearing a bear mask?
- Look at pages 6 and 7. What else do you think Uncle Ted could have put in the twins' socks that would have felt like worms?
- Look at pages 10 and 11. What do you think Mom would say if she saw the twins putting salt on Uncle Ted's ice cream?
- Look at page 14. Why do you think Uncle Ted is not angry with the twins? How do you know this?

EXPLORING LANGUAGE

Terminology

Title, cover, illustrations, author, illustrator

Vocabulary

Interest words: twins, mask, trick, salt, spoon
High-frequency words: play, ran, their, day, fast, from, one
Positional words: in, on, over

Print Conventions

Capital letter for sentence beginnings and names (**U**ncle **T**ed, **M**om), periods, commas, exclamation marks, quotation marks